This book belongs to

. . . .

. . . .

LONDON, NEW YORK, SYDNEY, PARIS,
MUNICH, and JOHANNESBURG

Written in consultation with child psychologist
Flora Hogman, Ph.D.

Senior Editor Linda Esposito
Senior Art Editor Diane Thistlethwaite
U.S. Editor Beth Sutinis
Production Chris Avgherinos and Silvia La Greca
Jacket Design Karen Shooter

First American Edition, 2001
Published in the United States by DK Publishing, Inc.
95 Madison Avenue, New York, NY 10016

2 4 6 8 10 9 7 5 3 1

Library of Congress Cataloging-in-Publication Data

Robbins, Beth.

Tom, Ally, and the babysitter / by Beth Robbins ; illustrated by Jon Stuart.– 1st American ed.
p. cm. -- (It's O.K.)
Summary: Tom's fear of the new babysitter begins to dissolve after she arrives and invites
Tom to play a game.
ISBN 0-7894-7427-1 -- ISBN 0-7894-7426-3 (pbk.)
[1. Babysitters--Fiction. 2. Fear--Fiction. 3. Cats--Fiction. 4. Rabbits--Fiction]
I. Stuart, Jon, ill. II. Title. III. Series.

PZ7.R53235 Ne2001
[E]--dc21   00-058940

Color reproduction by Colourscan, Singapore
Printed and bound by L.E.G.O. in Italy

see our complete
catalog at
www.dk.com

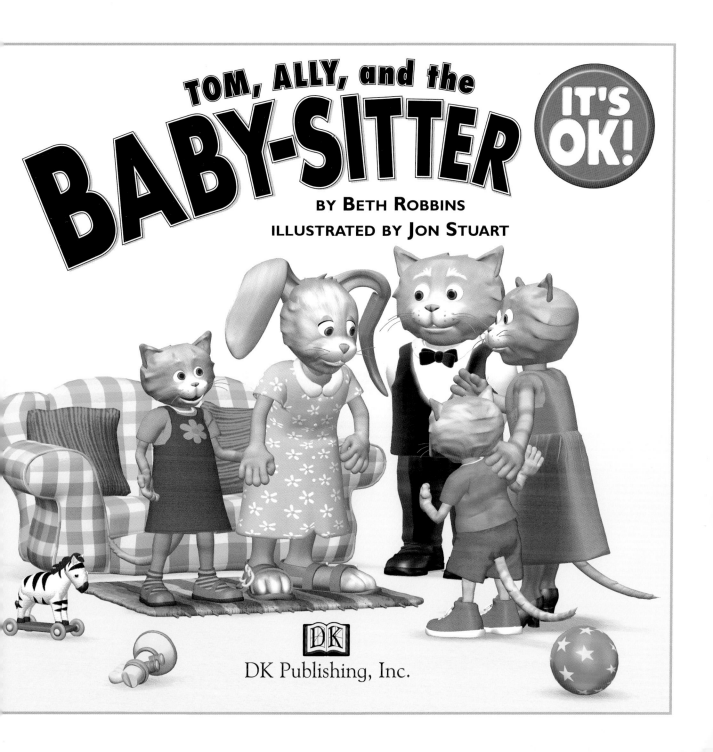

TOM, ALLY, and the BABY-SITTER

IT'S OK!

BY **BETH ROBBINS**

ILLUSTRATED BY **JON STUART**

DK Publishing, Inc.

"Why can't Granny stay with us?" asked Ally.
"She's busy tonight," said Mom.

"I don't need a baby-sitter,"
Tom grumbled.
"I'm not a baby!"

"This collar itches
and these pants
are too tight!"
moaned Dad.

Mom laughed.
"There's only one baby
in this house!" she said.
"And that's Dad!"

4

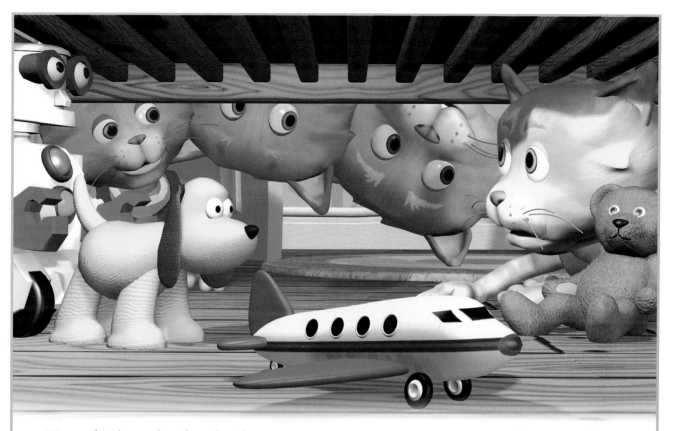

Tom hid under his bed.
Mom, Dad, and Ally tried to coax him out.

"Baby-sitters don't just take care of *babies*," said Mom.
"They take care of children of all ages," said Dad.

"Nora baby-sits my friend, Lily," said Ally. "You'll like Nora.
She's got long ears and the biggest feet you ever saw!"

"She sounds like a horrible monster!" cried Tom.

Tom's imagination started
running wild.

"Nora isn't a monster," said Mom.
"She's very nice!"

"She does have big feet though," joked Dad.
"Even bigger than mine!"

Tom tried to smile.
"I feel all strange inside," he said.

"You're probably just nervous,"
said Mom.
"Sometimes we get nervous
when we meet new people."

"What is a variety show?" asked Ally.
"It's a show with lots of different acts," said Mom.

"I want to come, too," said Tom, putting on Dad's jacket.
"And me," said Ally.

"No," said Dad. "We won't be home until very late."
"It's not fair!" Tom cried.

"We've still got half an hour before we leave," said Mom. "Why don't you put on your own show."

"We'll be the audience," said Dad.

Singer!

Comedian!

Dancers!

Jugglers!

SPLOSH!

12

"Calm down, kittens," said Mom.
"That's enough excitement for tonight!"

Dingdong!

"That must be the baby-sitter," said
Dad. And he went to answer the door.

"I want you to promise to be
on your best behavior tonight," said Mom.
"We promise," said the kittens.

"Please do exactly as Nora tells you,"
Mom said. "And remember your manners!"

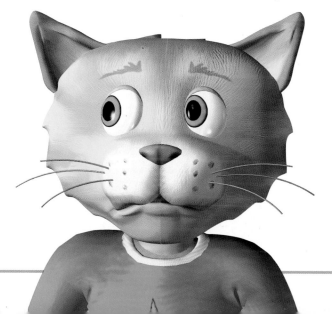

Tom could hear
loud footsteps in the hall.
He took a deep breath.

"I hope she's not a monster,"
he thought.

"Hello, Ally," said Nora.
Then she looked at Tom.
"Hello, you must be Tom," she smiled.

Tom felt his skin go bright red.

"Tom's shy!" Ally laughed.

"That's all right," said Nora.
"I get embarrassed when
I meet new people, too."

"There are cookies
in the cupboard," said Mom.
"But no more than two each."

"We've got chocolate milk, too!"
shouted Ally.

"Promise me that you will be
in bed by eight o'clock,"
said Dad.

The kittens grumbled.

"No arguments," said Mom.
"We promise," they said.

15

When it was time for
Mom and Dad to go,
Tom didn't want
them to leave.

Nora took him by the hand.
"Come on, Tom.
Let's play a game!"

"That sounds like fun,"
thought Tom.

"What would you kittens like to play?"
asked Nora.

"Hide-and-seek!" shouted the kittens,
waving good-bye to Mom and Dad.

Nora was "it."

She found Ally
in the laundry basket!

"Yuck!" said Nora.
"Smelly socks!"

17

It took a lot longer to find Tom.
They tried his bed,

behind the toy box,

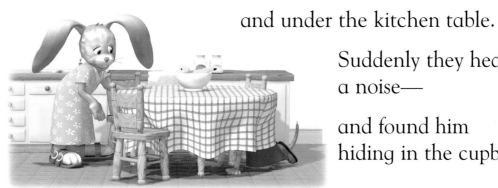

and under the kitchen table.

Suddenly they heard
a noise—

and found him
hiding in the cupboard.

Tom had eaten
all the cookies!

"I've got a tummy ache," groaned Tom.

"If you had done as you were told, you wouldn't feel so sick," said Nora.

"Ally, don't drink from the carton!"
said Nora. "It's bad manners."

"I don't care," Ally shouted.
"He ate all the cookies,
so I'll drink all the milk!"

"Two wrongs do not
make a right!" said Nora.

Tom tried to take
the carton away from Ally.

Nora tried to stop
the kittens from fighting.

In the scuffle,
milk spilled
all over
the kitchen.

"Look at this mess!" cried Nora.
"It's going to take me ages to clean it up."

Tom and Ally felt terrible.
"I'll help you," said Ally.

"I'll help, too,"
said Tom.

23

Together they cleaned up
the mess.
"Look," said Nora,
"this mop has a pair of ears
just like mine!"

Tom laughed. He liked Nora.
He could hardly believe he'd thought she was a monster.
Next time, he decided, he'd wait until he met someone
before deciding what they were like.

"If you two promise to behave from now on,
I'll read you a story," said Nora.

"We promise," said the kittens. And this time they really meant it.

Nora read them Tom's favorite dinosaur story.
"I think dinosaurs are scary," she said.

"I think they're funny," said Ally.

Tom thought for a moment.
"I'd like to meet one first before
making up my mind," he said.

Nora laughed.
"I think I can arrange that!" she said.

Using her long ears, Nora put on
a fantastic shadow show!

"Meet Tyrannosaurus Rex!"
said Nora.

"Diplodocus!"

"Pterodactyl!"

"Stegosaurus!"

"I hope Mom and Dad are
enjoying their show, too!"
said Ally.

In the theater, Dad had fallen asleep and was snoring loudly.
Mom was so embarrassed she turned pink!

Nora put Tom to bed first.
He was asleep as soon as
his head touched the pillow.

"It's almost eight o'clock," said Ally sleepily.
"I have to be in bed, too. I promised."

The next morning, Tom and Ally told Mom and Dad
all about the dinosaur show.

"I wish I'd seen that," said Dad. "Our show was boring."

"Nora promised to do bugs next time," said Ally.
"You'll have to go out soon, so she can baby-sit!" cried Tom.

"I don't think Mom wants to go out with me again," said Dad.
"Actually, I'd like to go to the movies next weekend," said Mom.
"Really?" said Dad. "What's playing?"
"Sleeping Beauty!" Mom laughed.